Annie Flies the Birthday Bike

by CRESCENT DRAGONWAGON

illustrated by EMILY ARNOLD McCULLY

Macmillan Publishing Company   New York   Maxwell Macmillan Canada   Toronto

Maxwell Macmillan International   New York   Oxford   Singapore   Sydney

Macmillan Publishing Company is part of the Maxwell Communication Group
of Companies.

Macmillan Publishing Company, 866 Third Avenue, New York, NY 10022.

Maxwell Macmillan Canada, Inc., 1200 Eglinton Avenue East, Suite 200, Don
Mills, Ontario M3C   3N1.

First Edition. Printed in the United States of America.
10   9   8   7   6   5   4   3   2   1

The text of this book is set in 16 pt. Garamond Book. The illustrations are
rendered in watercolor.

Library of Congress Cataloging-in-Publication Data
Dragonwagon, Crescent. Annie flies the birthday bike / by Crescent
Dragonwagon ; illustrated by Emily Arnold McCully.   p.   cm.
Summary: Annie gets the bicycle of her dreams for her birthday, but finds riding
it is harder than she thought. ISBN 0-02-733155-5
[1. Bicycles and bicycling—Fiction.   2. Birthdays—Fiction.]   I. McCully, Emily
Arnold, ill.   II. Title.
PZ7.D7824An   1993   [E]—dc20   90-42861

For Gina,
who knew, flew,
and will again, too.
Love,
C.D.

Two Weeks before Annie's Birthday

I don't ride that baby's trike. That's through.
I'd like a bike.
Blue, maybe. It's time for mine.

I can see me, flying free.
The boys fly down the hill;
when will I fly by, too?

Red or blue, silver spokes
past the Clays, past the Volks,
down Oak Place, like a race,
but me alone, road my own.
Fast time. Just mine.
Pedaling up, pushing hard,
fly past houses, past the yards
through the town, flying down.

"I think I'd like
a bike."

The Day of Annie's Birthday, Early

"Happy Birthday, dear Annie—"
I woke and thought, "Today!"
and lay in bed, just feeling it:
My birthday, still wrapped for me to open.

Envelopes, napkins tied with a bow
birthday breakfast down below
blueberry muffins, strawberry jam
scrambled eggs with cheese and ham
birthday-new stiff jeans, ten pockets,
swivel jump rope and a locket
green t-shirt with alligator:
please don't make me wait till later.

"All right, Annie, close your eyes—
not that this is a surprise."
Click-click-click, they wheel it in
click-click slowly, wheel's first spin—
It's blue, its name's in script in red,
it's a bicycle-bike, for me, it's blue—

"Well, do you like it, Annie?"
"Oh yes yes yes, I do I do!"

The Day of Annie's Birthday, Later

"Want to take a quick spin before school, Annie?"
My mother in a jogging suit, hair pulled back
driveway smooth and flat and black.

"Okay, I'll hold it, you can't fall,
I'll run, you pedal—"
    Is that *all*? Just *start*?
    My heart beats hard.
    But how?
    No training wheels,
    I told them,
    now it feels impossible
    to fly, to even *try*
    to move a little—

"Just try, Annie—push down! Good! Other foot! Good!
Okay! I'm here! I've got you—"
   Not easy. Not free. Scary. Harder than I thought
it would be, hard hard *hard*
in the driveway by the yard.

I'm not sure I even like—
what if I can't ever ride this bike?
The boys will laugh. What if I fall?
What made me ever think I could ride a bike at all?
"Annie, don't be discouraged, it just takes time. But
you'll get it, all at once, then you'll know how forever.
Promise. Annie?"
"Okay."

The Day after Annie's Birthday

"Mike Collins is going to push you one hour each day after school, Annie, until you get the hang of it."

Mike holds the bike, and me on it
His hair is red, his face is wet with sweat
from me riding, trying to ride
up and down back and forth
the block's longest flattest driveway (Mrs. Clay's)—

"Look, Annie, you'll get it,"
"Forget it," I want to say, "no way,"
    but Mrs. Clay is watching and I wanted a bike.
"Mike?"
"Yes, Annie?"
"Will I ever?"
"Yes, Annie."

Down and up, forth and back
bushes green, driveway black
Mike holding me on bike—
"Okay, Annie, call it a day. It happens
all at once, that's the way."
That's what they all say.

Six Days after Annie's Birthday

"How's the bike-riding coming, Annie?"
Well, it happened. Not all, but for a while:
Mike didn't hold me and I didn't fall.
Mike was there, still running,
but he took his hands off just a bit
and I didn't hit
the ground! Didn't go down!
Just a little way, today, but, I thought
someday…maybe someday—

"You have to keep trying, Annie, you did nearly six feet on your own,
you'll get it."
    Mike, less wet, less red, less running;
    it's a long way from flying.
"I went nearly six feet without Mike holding, nearly six feet."

A Week after Annie's Birthday

"Mrs. Clay says you did it, Annie!"
  Yes, it—
  I can't explain
  the bike stood up
  and I balanced and pedaled

it rained just a little but I didn't care
I bicycled, bicycled, in the wet air!
I wobbled a little, but I didn't fall
I went down the driveway and all the way back
and Mike shouting, "Yay! You did it today!"
I couldn't believe it, the way it worked, all
of it, all—and I didn't fall!
"Yes, I *did* do it—four whole times up and down Mrs. Clay's
driveway!"

Ten Days after Annie's Birthday

"Are you all right, Annie?"
    Well,
    I fell.

I cried. And you can see,
they put that red stuff on my knee
But it's okay, just hurts a little now.
Well, I fell, and this is how:

I went way way way to the top of the hill
and maybe I shouldn't have but I did,
and the bike rode itself, that's all I can say,
and the wind in my hair, and the flying-by air
and the going-down-no-pedal-I-wasn't-there
and then I got scared and started braking—
Mr. Volk was outside in his yard, he was raking.

I fell and he saw and came running, came flying
I was down on the pavement, lying there crying

and I hurt and I bled, on my elbow and knee
and he washed me and put on a Band-Aid—you see?

And it hurt and it still does, but now it's okay
because
I knew. I flew.
I will again, too.
"Yes, I'm all right, I really am."